MELOWY

The Secret Book

Danielle Star

Scholastic Inc.

Published by Scholastic Inc., *Publishers since 1920*,
557 Broadway, New York, NY 10012. SCHOLASTIC and associated logos
are trademarks and/or registered trademarks of Scholastic Inc.

ISBN 978-1-338-28171-2

Text by Danielle Star
Original title *Il libro segreto*
Editorial cooperation by Carolina Capria and Mariella Martucci
Illustrations by Erika De Pieri, Nicoletta Baldari, Barbara Bargiggia, Emilio Urbano, and Patrizia Zangrilli
Graphics by Danielle Stern

Special thanks to Tiffany Colón
Translated by Chris Turner
Interior design by Baily Crawford

10 9 8 7 6 5 4 3 2 1   18 19 20 21 22

Printed in the U.S.A.   40
First printing 2018

Contents

Imagine a magical land wrapped in golden light. A planet in a distant galaxy beyond the known stars. This enchanted place is known as Aura, and it is very special. For Aura is home to the pegasus, a winged horse with a colorful mane and coat.

The pegasuses of Aura come from four ancient island realms that lie within Aura's enchanted oceans: the Winter Realm of Amethyst Island, the Spring Realm of Emerald Island, the Day Realm of Ruby Island, and the Night Realm of Sapphire Island.

A selected number from each realm are born with a symbol on their wings and a hidden magical power. These are the Melowies.

When their magic beckons them in a dream, all Melowies leave their island homes to answer the call. They must attend school at the Castle of Destiny, a legendary castle hidden in a sea of clouds, where they will learn all about their hidden powers. Destiny is a place where friendships are born, where Melowies find their courage, and where they discover the true magic inside themselves!

Map of Aura

The Winter Realm

Map of the Castle of Destiny

1 Butterfly Tower—first-year dormitory

2 Dragonfly Tower—second-year dormitory

3 Swallow Tower—third-year dormitory

4 Eagle Tower—fourth-year dormitory

5 Principal Gia's office

6 Library

7 Classrooms

8 The Winter Tower

9 The Spring Tower

10 The Day Tower

11 The Night Tower

12 Waterfall

13 Runway

14 Assembly hall

15 Garden

16 Sports fields

17 Cafeteria

18 Kitchen

19 Auditorium

Meet the Melowies

Cleo

Her realm: unknown
Her personality: impulsive and loyal
Her passion: writing
Her gift: something mysterious . . .

Electra

Her realm: Day
Her personality: boisterous and bubbly
Her passion: fashion
Her gift: the Power of Light

Maya

Her realm: Spring
Her personality: shy and sweet
Her passion: cooking
Her gift: the Power of Heat

Cora

Her realm: Winter
Her personality: proud and sincere
Her passion: ice-skating
Her gift: the Power of Cold

Selena

Her realm: Night
Her personality: deep and sensitive
Her passion: music
Her gift: the Power of Darkness

1
The Legend of the Scorpion

The sun was shining brightly just beyond the clouds that surround the Castle of Destiny like an ocean of whipped cream. The rays shone through the castle windows, and a gentle breeze filled the garden. Everything seemed to glow on that special day. Everything except Cleo's mood.

The Harmony Festival was going to start in just a few hours, and she was not interested in joining her friends Selena, Maya, Cora, and Electra. She might have felt a little better if Theodora was there to cheer her up, but the school cook was busy preparing thousands of delicious goodies for the festival.

Cleo decided the next best thing was a book. Sometimes a

really good book can lift your mood almost as well as a good friend. Cleo climbed the steps to the library with its gleaming windows and walls covered with books.

"I would like to borrow a book, please," she said as she walked into the library. Suddenly, she realized Ms. Circe, the librarian, was nowhere to be found. Snobby Eris stood behind the desk, smiling.

"Which book would you like?" Eris asked.

"Eris! What are you doing here?" Cleo asked.

"Ms. Circe is busy running an errand and asked me to fill in for her here. Hurry up, choose your book, and scram."

"Wow, that's really rude," Cleo answered.

"Whenever you and your little friends are around, I get in trouble. Don't think I have forgotten about the punishment I got all because of you." Eris still trembled with rage at the thought of the hours she had to spend in the kitchen helping Theodora after she tried to ruin the survival test in the Neon Forest.

"That was your own fault!" Cleo said. "Anyway, washing a few dishes never hurt anybody."

"A few dishes?!" Eris cried. "It was way more than a few! I also had to peel so many potatoes that I'll never be able to look at another one for as long as I live. Anyway, which book do you want? Pick something and get out of here."

"I don't know, exactly. A good adventure story, maybe?"

"I have just what you're looking for." Eris

walked to the closet where Ms. Circe kept her stuff and opened the drawer of an old cabinet. She pulled out a book with a stained cover. The pages were damp, as if someone had been reading it in the shower. Eris found it while she was snooping through Ms. Circe's things and assumed it was in this pile because no one wanted to borrow it. It must have been the worst book in the library.

"What is it?" Cleo asked.

"Take it and find out for yourself. It's called

The Legend of the Scorpion. Maybe it's a fantasy? One of those boring stories where the bad guy loses and the good guy wins." Eris threw the book at Cleo. As she did, something fell out from between its pages and landed on the floor with a clatter. Eris picked it up carefully.

"Is it a bookmark?" Cleo asked.

"It looks like it," Eris responded. The bookmark was silver and seemed to be decorated with strange symbols and the image of a scorpion. Eris slipped it back into Ms. Circe's drawer.

Cleo was walking out of the library when Eris stopped her. "Hang on. I have to record it in the log."

"Sorry, I forgot," Cleo said. She was in a

big hurry to get back to her room and start reading. She handed the book to Eris, who recorded it in Biblioscan, the computer program.

"You do know that scorpions are dangerous, don't you?" Eris asked after scanning the book into the computer. "Whack! One flick of its tail and it's good-bye to you." She leaned toward Cleo and imitated a scorpion sting with her hoof.

Cleo shivered.

"Don't be such a scaredy-cat." Eris laughed. "I was only joking."

"You're about as funny as a stubbed toe," Cleo said.

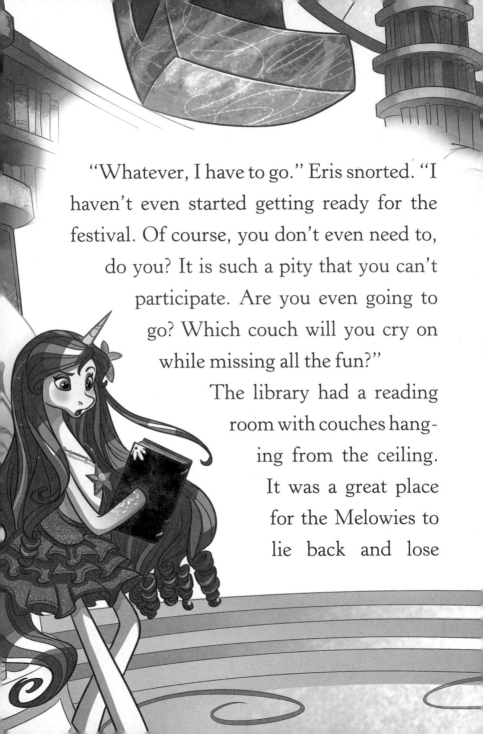

"Whatever, I have to go." Eris snorted. "I haven't even started getting ready for the festival. Of course, you don't even need to, do you? It is such a pity that you can't participate. Are you even going to go? Which couch will you cry on while missing all the fun?"

The library had a reading room with couches hanging from the ceiling. It was a great place for the Melowies to lie back and lose

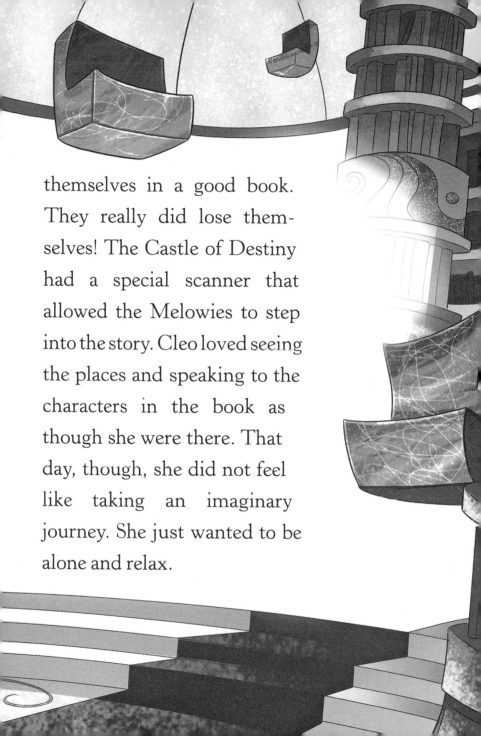

themselves in a good book. They really did lose themselves! The Castle of Destiny had a special scanner that allowed the Melowies to step into the story. Cleo loved seeing the places and speaking to the characters in the book as though she were there. That day, though, she did not feel like taking an imaginary journey. She just wanted to be alone and relax.

"I'm going back to my room, Eris."

"Whatever, enjoy the book," Eris said with a sneer.

Just a few minutes later, Ms. Circe came back from the store. "Did anyone stop by while I was away?" she asked Eris.

"Yes, and I gave her just the book she was searching for," said Eris. "Can I go now?"

Ms. Circe nodded, and Eris rushed to get ready for the celebration.

As soon as she was sure she was alone, the librarian opened her private drawer and was shocked! *Where was* The Legend of the Scorpion?! *That silly Melowy couldn't have taken it; she hates reading! She must have let someone take it out of the library!*

Ms. Circe signed into Biblioscan to find
out who that someone was.

2
A Beautiful Gift

Cleo went back to her dormitory, flew up to her bed, lay down, and opened the book. From the very first page, *The Legend of the Scorpion* was a creepy story. The illustrations were even creepier. They were full of scorpions with scary eyes, shiny claws, and sharp stingers that were ready to ooze poison.

Cleo couldn't stop reading! Maybe it was because the story was so exciting, or because the pages were decorated with strange symbols along the edges that looked like the alphabet from an ancient language. It was as though the book had some strange power over her. She felt like she had fallen into a pool of thick, gooey liquid that she couldn't pull herself out of.

Suddenly, a noise made her jump. Someone had opened the door, and a strong gust of wind blew into the room. She dropped the book, and it fell onto the floor.

"Hi, Cleo!" Cora cried. "You look like you've just seen a ghost!"

Cleo sighed with relief at seeing her friends. "Sorry, I just lost myself in a book," she said. "You all look so beautiful!" she exclaimed, seeing their glamorous dresses for the festival.

"Why haven't you started getting ready yet?" exclaimed Electra. "The ceremony starts in half an hour!"

Cleo stared at her friends. They were all wearing beautiful new outfits, each one perfectly reflecting the realm they came from. Electra had on a soft silk scarf that seemed

to shine as though it was bathed in sunlight. Cora's dress glowed with different colors like the sky lit up by the northern lights. Selena's dress was dotted with shining stars, while Maya had a flouncy skirt that looked like it had been woven out of flowers.

Cleo felt embarrassed and said nothing.

"Come on!" Electra cried. "Hurry up and get ready! What are you reading anyway?" She picked the book up from the floor. "Lethal scorpions, poisonous princesses . . . that's enough! You'd better hurry up and get dressed, instead of reading this creepy book."

"And wear what?" asked Cleo with a gloomy expression. "I don't know where I am from, so I don't have anything to wear."

"Oh, poor you," Electra teased. "Maybe instead of reading that weird book, you should read *Cinderella*. She didn't have a dress to wear, either, and she ended up the belle of the ball."

"Show her the present!" Maya said. "That will definitely cheer her up!"

Electra left the room and came back with a huge smile on her face and the most beautiful dress Cleo had ever seen. And it was just for her!

"But—but I—I," Cleo stammered. She could hardly speak she was so surprised.

"I designed it and made it special for you," Electra said. "After lunch and before afternoon classes, I have been locking myself up in the workshop, and with a little help from Ms. Eros, I sewed it! I'm really happy with how it came out. What do you think, Cleo?"

"I have never seen anything so beautiful in my whole life," Cleo cried, filled with wonder and gratitude. "Well, what are you waiting for?" asked Selena. "Put it on!" "Electra, I don't know how to thank you. You are such a wonderful friend."

Cleo put on the dress. Her friends crowded around her in a colorful circle. Cleo didn't need a mirror to know how she looked. She could see from the way her friends were staring at her that the dress fit perfectly.

The Melowies were all so enchanted by Cleo's new dress that no one noticed Maya looking at the book lying on the ground. She picked it up and started flipping through the pages, growing more and more interested with every page. She loved animals; it didn't matter if they were cats, dogs, or scorpions. "I would really like to read this book, too," she muttered.

"I'll lend it to you when I am done," Cleo said.

But Maya didn't answer. She couldn't take her eyes off the pages. Maybe the book did have some strange powers.

3
Melowy Hip-Hop

"I am very excited to be celebrating Aura's Harmony Festival once again!" Principal Gia said. Her voice got lost from time to time, drowned out by the sound of Melowies splashing in the waterfall in the garden where all the students had assembled.

"Blah, blah, blah," Maya whispered to Selena. "How long is this speech?"

"I don't know," Selena answered.

"Well, I'm already bored," Maya said with a sigh. "What a drag!"

Selena was surprised. Maya adored Principal Gia and usually hung on her every word. Plus, she was always so kind and respectful. Being so rebellious was very out of character for her.

"Let's remember that one of the values that inspires our teaching here is harmony. The other five core values of the Castle of Destiny are selflessness . . ."

"Yeah, yeah, justice, dialogue, peace," Maya whispered to her friends. "Like we don't already know this!"

"Well, some of us still haven't learned them," Electra whispered, looking at Eris, who was in the next row giggling with her friends Leda and Kate.

"Hey, Cleo, are you listening?" Cora asked, gently nudging her friend. "You seem more interested in the bushes."

Cleo pulled herself out of her thoughts. She had been staring at the bright red berries that dotted the hedge. She'd been feeling strange since she left the room. It was like the splashing of the waterfall and the breeze were clouding her thoughts.

"Oh, sorry, Cora. I am just having a hard time paying attention. Maybe I am a little tired."

There was a round of applause when Principal Gia finished her speech.

"Now the fun can start!" Cora said.

"And now," Principal Gia continued, "Ms. Calliope will teach you some of the traditional magic dances of Aura." There was another round of applause.

"Oh no!" grumbled Maya. "I can't stand traditional dances."

"What is wrong with you today?" Electra asked. "Have you eaten nettles or something?"

The third-year orchestra took its place in the garden surrounded by asters, the special flower that grew all around the Castle of Destiny. They looked like big pink daisies with thick, rubbery petals like candied sugar. Ben, the school's strange but wise gardener, had given them the power to react to sound. As soon as the orchestra started playing, their petals shook back and forth, and their stems swayed in time with the music.

The students gathered around Ms. Calliope while she danced in circles that got smaller and smaller like the image in a kaleidoscope.

Maya is right, Cora thought after a few spins, *this dance is very boring.* The others seemed to feel the same way as they just stood around and watched.

Ms. Ariadne knew her students well and made a suggestion no one could refuse. "How about some Melowy hip-hop?" she asked.

"Oh yeah!" all of the students cried out at once.

The orchestra began playing a pounding rhythm and the poor asters started shaking their petals at a quick pace. All of the Melowies started dancing. Ms. Calliope joined in, too, her cheeks turning the color of tomatoes from the effort.

Mr. Cratos, the art teacher, saved her by interrupting the dance for an announcement.

4
The Rainbow Slide

"Dear students, on this exciting occasion, it makes me very happy to . . . ," Mr. Cratos began. But, as usual, he started to mumble and his words got all tangled up. No one could understand anything he was saying. The Melowies tried to keep themselves from giggling.

Mr. Cratos was a very talented artist, but he was not very good with words, and he

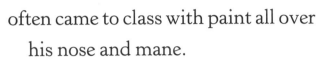

often came to class with paint all over his nose and mane.

"I've always thought he was a lovely teacher," said Maya, who had a real soft spot for him. "But he sounds so silly up there. Why doesn't he just buy a dictionary?"

Cora nodded. Her friend did have a point, but it was strange for Maya to say something so mean. Finally, Mr. Cratos finished his speech, and Principal Gia stepped in.

"And now girls, how about we all take a dip?" she asked, with a beaming smile. "After that, we can all enjoy the delicious buffet Theodora has prepared!"

The principal rang her bell, and the students all squealed in excitement. They had all been waiting for this moment. Whenever she rang that bell, they knew that something special was about to happen. Sure enough, a huge rainbow suddenly appeared, forming a waterslide into the fountain below!

All of the fillies' clothes turned into beautiful swimsuits that perfectly matched their wings and manes. They all rushed toward the slide and formed a line.

"WOW!" Electra yelled when it was her turn. Daring as ever, she threw herself down on her belly. *"This is fun!"*

Cleo and Selena went down the slide together. Cora and Maya went next, close behind them. They ended up sending a big

wave over Cleo and Selena just as they were coming up for air. Suddenly, another big wave went right over their heads.

A small, furry creature swam to the edge of the pool, climbed out, and shook the water off.

"Fluffy!" Selena laughed. "I thought you hated water!"

Theodora rushed over to pick up the dog.

"I told you not to dive in, you little rascal! You'll give yourself a cold!" she said as she dried off Fluffy's fur with her kitchen towel.

"The buffet is ready!" she announced to the crowd of Melowies.

Their swimsuits transformed back into beautiful evening gowns as the girls protested. "Just one more turn on the slide, please!"

"I am pretty hungry, though," Cleo said, walking over to the buffet. The swim had cleared her head a little, but she was still feeling a bit strange. Her brain was fuzzy, and it seemed as though the rest of the world was blurry and muffled.

Eris and her friends, Kate and Leda, pulled her back to reality when they pushed in front of everyone else in line to stack their plates high with all the food they could lay their hooves on. It did not really matter. Theodora had made so much food that there was plenty for everyone. There were pizzas, fries, popcorn, tacos, fruit tarts, chocolate cakes, and yummy candies shaped like pegasuses.

"Theodora, everything tastes so delicious!" all the students told her. "It must have taken you forever to prepare all of this food!"

Theodora, with the dripping-wet Fluffy up on one shoulder, was as proud as could be, but pretended it was nothing. "Oh, this was no big deal! I was able to pull it all together pretty quickly!" she said.

Then it was time to cut the cake. Mr. Zelus appeared, flying through the air holding the biggest cake any of them had ever seen, all frosted with delicate pastel colors. It was a model of the Castle of Destiny with details drawn on with cream, sugar, and chocolate marking pens. When Principal Gia cut the first slice, all the Melowies erupted in thunderous applause. Theodora helped her cut the rest so that all of the students could help themselves to some.

Everyone was given some pegasus pop, a drink with tiny pink bubbles that tasted like strawberry, orange, and pomegranate. It was something the Melowies only drank on very special occasions.

Even after the toast and the cake, Cleo still felt strange. Maya sounded even stranger. "I'm sorry, I've smudged my lip gloss. I'm going back to our room for a minute to redo my makeup."

Cleo watched her walk away. "But Maya loves

cake. I have never seen her turn down sweet snacks. Why would she leave her piece here to reapply some lip gloss? Something isn't adding up."

5
Has Anyone Seen Maya?

The older Melowies were having lots of fun telling the girls all about the school's secrets.

"Ms. Ariadne seems really strict, but all you have to do is win her over. She'll love you forever if you're kind and you work really hard. She might even remember your name!"

"Mr. Zelus is strict, too, but he has a couple of favorites," their classmates were saying.

"That's not true!" another Melowy said.

"It is, too, true. You're just saying that because you're one of his favorites." The Melowy giggled.

Cleo stood in the circle and listened while she looked around for Maya. *She's been gone a long time,* she thought. *Why isn't she back yet? What is she up to?*

"Selena," Cleo said, trying to get her friend's attention. But Selena was so into the conversation she didn't hear.

"Electra! Cora!" But her other friends were just as interested in the secrets of the castle.

So Cleo walked off, staring at the ground with a gloomy expression. She noticed that the asters seemed to be staring straight at

her. Then, something very strange happened. One of the flowers turned toward
her and pointed into the castle with its thick
petals.

"I'm not feeling well today." Cleo shook
her head. "My imagination is playing tricks
on me." She blinked a few times, trying to
snap out of it. Then she noticed someone
else was watching her.

"There is some-
thing wonderful
about everything
in nature," Ben,
the gardener,
said. His voice
blended in with
the happy sounds

of the laughing and chatting from the party. Cleo stared at him blankly.

"That's what the ancient sages of Aura say," Ben continued. "I didn't know how special you were, young lady, but you are. Asters only speak to very special souls, and even then, it is very rare. In fact, I have only seen it happen a few times in my whole life. That flower just spoke to you."

"It spoke to me?" Cleo asked, amazed. "The flower?" She certainly didn't feel unique, just weird.

"Don't think too much about it, Cleo. Just listen to the messages nature is sending you."

Ben was a bit odd, but he really did know a lot about plants. He wasn't just the

gardener, he was also the school's botany teacher. There was no mistaking it, the aster was definitely pointing to the castle. Maybe it wanted Cleo to go inside?

She trotted back to her friends. This time she grabbed Electra and pulled her away from the rest of the group. "Maya went back to the room to fix her makeup," Cleo whispered. "It isn't like her to leave a buffet before she has had her fill of cake. She said she was coming right back, but that was a long time ago. Have you seen her?"

"No," Electra said. "I guess I didn't even notice when she left."

"Don't you think she has been acting a little strange all day? She's making nasty comments about everything and everyone," Cleo continued.

"Yes, I did notice that," Electra said with a worried expression. "I just thought she was in a bad mood."

Electra went over to get the other girls.

"Aww, you guys are ruining the party! Why do we have to go back to the room?" Cora asked as the friends walked up the spiral staircase back to Butterfly Tower. "We were having so much fun!"

"Haven't you realized Maya is missing? We have to go find her," Electra answered.

6
The Masked Creature

"Maya!" Electra called down the hall. "Where are you?"

She stopped at the door and peeked inside. Everything looked exactly as they had left it. There was a strange noise that drowned out all the happy sound coming from the garden. It sounded like a thousand tiny claws snapping open and shut.

Electra, Selena, Cora, and Cleo were on high alert, and for some reason, they all felt afraid. Very cautiously they walked into the room. What they found was worse than they could have imagined.

Maya was laying against the wall in the far corner of the room with *The Legend of the Scorpion* lying open on her stomach. Her eyes were closed, and she wasn't moving. It looked like she had fainted. Worse than that, her whole body was covered in a swarming blanket of scorpions.

A creature dressed in black suddenly appeared in the middle of the room. It was wearing a creepy scorpion mask that covered its entire face.

"Cleo, my dear," it said in a strangely persuasive, soft voice, "come here."

Cleo didn't move a muscle. She was frozen to her spot!

"This book was yours, wasn't it?" the creature asked, moving toward her. "Maya took it from you without asking permission.

Some friend she turned out to be! As I always say, there is no such thing as true friendship. I thought you would want her to be punished for her crime. Are you happy?"

Where have I seen that mask before? Cleo wondered. She couldn't remember because her thoughts were spinning out of control.

The masked creature took the book from Maya's stomach and shook off the scorpions. Something silver glinted in the sunlight.

Just then she remembered the bookmark that fell out of *The Legend of the Scorpion.* "That's the scorpion I saw on the bookmark!" she cried.

"That book is evil!" exclaimed Electra. "Look what it's done to Maya!"

"The symbols along the edges of the pages must be magic spells," Cleo mumbled. "I felt weird after I read them, and I still don't feel right. Eris gave me that book!"

"Eris?" Selena asked angrily. "Don't tell me she's mixed up in this, too! That horrible Melowy has some serious explaining to do."

"Enough! I am sick of all your talk!" the creature shouted, turning to Maya. "You all need to be taught a lesson for sticking your noses in business that doesn't concern you. Prepare to face the wrath of the scorpion."

The creature opened the book and began reading one of the magic spells. The scorpions began to march toward Maya's face, their stingers at the ready.

7

Frozen in Fear

Down at the festival, Melowies began to notice the group of friends was missing.

"Where are they?" asked Ruby, a sophomore Melowy with an auburn mane. "They said they were going back to their room for a minute, but that was ages ago."

"Who cares?" Eris grumbled with a shrug. She couldn't believe how lucky she was. Her rivals, who were always so popular with teachers and going on and on about what great friends they were, had left the festival. This gave her the chance to win the older students over. She wasn't going to let this opportunity slip away.

"Maybe we should go look for them," Ruby said. She looked worried.

"I don't think that's a very good idea," Leda answered. "If we wander off from such an important event, Principal Gia could get very angry. I don't want to get on her bad side."

"I guess you are right," Ruby said. "But what could they be doing up there? Giving a millipede a manicure?"

Meanwhile, back in their room, the friends stood as still as statues. They were too afraid to move.

A scorpion started crawling up Maya's cheek. Seeing the dangerous creature getting ready to strike gave the girls a courage they didn't know they had. They had to do something to help Maya, fast!

Electra concentrated all of the light she could find inside herself and was ready to blast the scorpion with her powers, but she stopped herself. She was worried she would burn her friend as well.

Cora had learned how to make beautiful ice sculptures and freeze things, but there was no teacher here looking out for her. This was real life. What if she got it wrong and froze her friend in a block of ice, too? What would happen then?

Selena closed her eyes. Her power of darkness came from a place of deep inner calm, but she was feeling anything but calm. As a child she could play with shadows, imagining they were living things. Where were those shadow creatures now that she needed them most?

Cleo felt more helpless than any of them. She didn't have a burning light inside her like Electra. She couldn't freeze things in their tracks like Cora. She couldn't turn darkness into fantastic creatures the way Selena could. She didn't have a clue what she could do to help!

While Cleo was giving in to her doubts, the scorpion arched its tail getting ready to strike.

8
The Power of All Powers

The Melowies stared at the scorpion with wide eyes.

Cleo was so focused on the creature about to sting her friend that she didn't notice her wings had started to glow. The light shifted, concentrating around her horn. Suddenly, a flash of a thousand colors lit up everything in the room.

In stunned silence, the other Melowies stared at their friend standing before them. The light around her was so dazzling that they could no longer see her. Cleo, who had always longed to know which realm her power came from, had just created a blast of energy as powerful as the light of a star.

"Cleo!" Electra shouted as she realized she couldn't hold back the light inside her. A powerful ray of light shot out from her horn and destroyed the scorpion in an instant.

Cora felt her power growing stronger and stronger. In a flash, she froze all of the other scorpions into one big block.

"How dare you, you silly fillies!" roared the masked creature. "If a few scorpions don't scare you, let's see how you handle a swarm of them!" With a chilling laugh, it pointed the silver bookmark at them.

At the very same time, Selena clapped her wings together three times. The shadow of an enormous wolf appeared in the room. It

bared its fangs and growled a noise that shook the walls. The masked creature shrieked with terror and disappeared through the door.

The Melowies stared at one another, amazed at their own powers. Most of all, they were amazed by Cleo. The extraordinary light she created surrounded them all and completely took away all their doubts, making them stronger than ever. The magical rainbow that Cleo created helped them find the courage to believe in themselves and save Maya.

"That was amazing!" Electra said. "Maybe that is your power Cleo. A power that makes others stronger. It's some sort of energy that brings others together in harmony."

The Melowies heard voices in the corridor outside their room. Principal Gia and Ben appeared in the room. "We were wondering where you fillies had gone to," the principal said rather sternly while looking around. The room now looked entirely normal. "It's bad manners to leave a ceremony for so long. Do you find the festival boring?"

"I would say the last couple of hours have been anything but boring," Electra said, just getting over her amazement. She told the principal and the gardener everything about the book, the mysterious masked figure, the spell, and how Cleo was able to make her friends' powers stronger than they'd ever been.

Principal Gia listened with a serious expression and looked at Cleo's pendant. It was glowing as if it were red hot. It was because of the pendant that she was not affected by the evil book the way Maya was. Cleo, the Melowy without a realm, had finally found her power.

"Cleo, I am so proud of you," she said, her voice full of emotion. "Without your help, something terrible might have happened here today."

Maya finally opened her eyes and looked around the room, bewildered. "What happened?" she asked.

The Melowies ran over to hug her.

Principal Gia looked happy and proud. But a shadow was clouding her thoughts. Who was the masked creature? How was it able to get into the school? For better or worse, something had happened that day that would change the castle forever.

Epilogue

The festival was finally over, and the library was wrapped in the silence of the night. The books were nestled in their shelves, and the Melowies were resting in their beds.

A single ray of moonlight shone through the high windows lighting up the only one still awake at that hour as she wandered restlessly up and down the aisles of books.

"What will the Supreme Ruler say when she hears I almost lost the book?" Ms. Circe muttered to herself. "That book is so important for the final attack."

Ms. Circe clutched the silver bookmark, which would help her cast her magic spells. "Gia," she whispered, "your days here are numbered."

See how it all began! Read the first exciting moment in the Melowies' journey:

Dreams Come True

The Big Day

Something very special was happening. Way up in the sky above the land of Aura, a magical trail had appeared in the clouds. It would only remain there for one day. Twenty-four pairs of wings fluttered in the cool air. Twenty-four silky manes sparkled in the morning light. Today was the big day. The day the Melowies were going to the Castle of Destiny for the first time!

Maya flapped her pink wings. She'd left

her home in the Spring Realm and was now flying with a bunch of other special pegasuses to the place they'd all dreamed about since they were little. She was so excited to finally find out more about her magic! It was just a shame that she was too shy to share her excitement with the others. But maybe, with a little effort . . .

Maya spotted a group of girls giggling nearby. She took a deep breath, flew over to them, and summoned her courage. "Hi, girls! How are you?" she whispered. The words were so soft that the others didn't hear. They glided away on a whistling air current without even noticing her.

Feeling disappointed, Maya watched them flying off into the distance. But then she noticed a pegasus with a purple mane who was floating all by herself. Maya flew over to her with a flutter of wings. "HELLO! WHAT'S YOUR NAME?" she said, this time far too loudly.

The stranger looked her up and down. In a flat voice, she answered, "Selena."

"I'm Maya. Umm . . . are you a Melowy, too?" Maya asked, trying to make conversation.

"Of course," the pretty pegasus replied.

Now Maya felt silly. Selena had to be a Melowy! Only Melowies, the pegasuses born with a symbol on their wings and a hidden magical power, could go where they were going.

Selena gave her a sideways look. Did Maya

know how important this journey was? Selena wasn't trying to be nasty. But she usually liked to be alone and wanted to enjoy the special moment without distractions. Besides, Selena wasn't used to being around other Melowies. At home, in her mother's castle, she was the only one she'd ever known.

Suddenly, an "Ooh!" echoed along the path through the clouds. The Melowy who had been flying at the front of the herd, Cora from the Winter Realm, suddenly seemed to lose her perfect poise. Her blue eyes grew wide with wonder as she gazed at what lay ahead.

The Melowies saw an island floating in the middle of a sea of clouds! The island was crowned by a beautiful castle with soaring towers surrounded by homes and other buildings below. It was the Castle of Destiny, the school for Melowies. And it was just as Cora had always imagined it! She'd been waiting to come here since she was a tiny pegasus, and finally, her time had come. She wanted everything to be perfect.

"Wings out, chin up, look proud," she said to herself as she recovered her composure and followed the last stretch of the sparkling path through the clouds. She took a deep breath. "Wings out, chin—"

"*Coming through!*" someone suddenly yelled from behind her.

EXPLORE DESTINY WITH THE MELOWIES AS THEY DISCOVER THEIR MAGICAL POWERS!

Hidden somewhere beyond the highest clouds is the Castle of Destiny, a school for very special students. They're the Melowies, young pegasuses born with a symbol on their wings and a hidden magical power. And the time destined for them to meet has now arrived.

■SCHOLASTIC
scholastic.com

MELOWY6